Sweet
BABY
Cakes

Written & Illustrated By

ARIANA MOORE

REDEMPTION PRESS

Published by Redemption Press, PO Box 427, Enumclaw, WA 98022.
Toll-Free (844) 2REDEEM (273-3336)

Redemption Press is honored to present this title in partnership with the author. The views expressed or implied in this work are those of the author. Redemption Press provides our imprint seal representing design excellence, creative content, and high-quality production.

The author has tried to recreate events, locales, and conversations from memories of them. In order to maintain their anonymity, in some instances the names of individuals, some identifying characteristics, and some details may have been changed, such as physical properties, occupations, and places of residence.

All Scripture quotations are taken from The Holy Bible, English Standard Version® (ESV®) © 2001 by Crossway, a publishing ministry of Good News Publishers. All rights reserved.

ISBN 13: 978-1-64645-774-8 (Paperback)
978-1-64645-773-1 (ePub)

Library of Congress Catalog Card Number: 2023916541

Dedicated with much love to my sweet four:

Calvin, Natalie, Jed and Breck

Attach photo of Mama and Baby here.

Baby Cakes, Sugarplum, Cupcake, Sweetie Pie—

these terms of endearment remind me of your precious beginnings.

Long before you were born, I loved you.

And I counted down the weeks until I could meet you,

my sweet baby.

When you were smaller than a single sugar crystal,

every detail was already perfectly designed:

your face, the color of your hair,

whether you'd be a boy or a girl.

I couldn't wait to learn everything about you!

And you grew and grew until you were the size of a sprinkle! Even when you were that tiny, your heart was already beating and pumping blood. Just knowing your heart was growing made my own heart grow with an overwhelming love.

Attach first sonogram photo here.

And you grew and grew until you were the size of a piece of candy! By then, all your beautiful features were already formed: your eyes, ears, nose and mouth. I couldn't wait to see you face to face!

And you grew and grew until you were the size of a cookie! I went to the doctor to check in on you. A special machine let me hear your heartbeat. That sweet whooshing sound made my own heart—so close to yours—pitter-patter with love. I was so thankful to be your mommy!

And you grew and grew, from the size of a cookie to a doughnut to a cupcake! If you weren't sleeping or stretching or yawning or sucking your thumb, you were busy kicking. It was like you were saying, "Hey, Mommy! Want to play?" Sometimes you'd wake me up in the middle of the night, kicking! Even when you were that small, you were so much fun!

And you grew and grew until you were the size of an ice cream cone! I went to the doctor's office for an extra sweet visit. The doctor rolled a special wand over my tummy and captured an image of YOU inside ME! I never saw anything quite so beautiful.

Attach sonogram photo here.

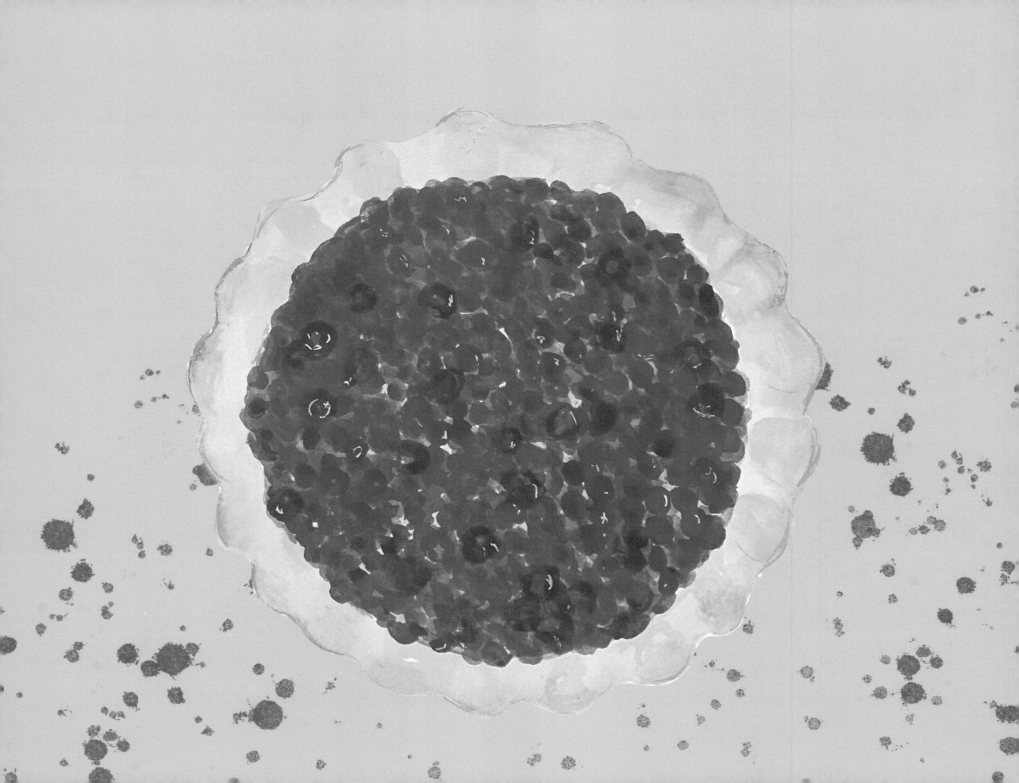

And you grew and grew

from the size of an ice cream cone

to a pie . . .

Sweet Baby Cakes

. . . until it was finally your BIRTHday!

What JOY it was to be face to face with my sweet gift!

One day you will be fully grown, but my love for you will never stop growing! And you'll always be my Sweet Baby Cakes!

Attach photo of your newborn here.

"For you formed my inward parts; you knitted me together in my mother's womb. I praise you, for I am fearfully and wonderfully made. Wonderful are your works; my soul knows it very well."

Psalm 139:13–14

ORDER INFORMATION

To order additional copies of this book, please visit
www.redemption-press.com.
Also available at Christian bookstores, Amazon, and Barnes and Noble.

Printed in the USA
CPSIA information can be obtained
at www.ICGtesting.com
CBHW040028110824

12905CB00063B/372